Brownies

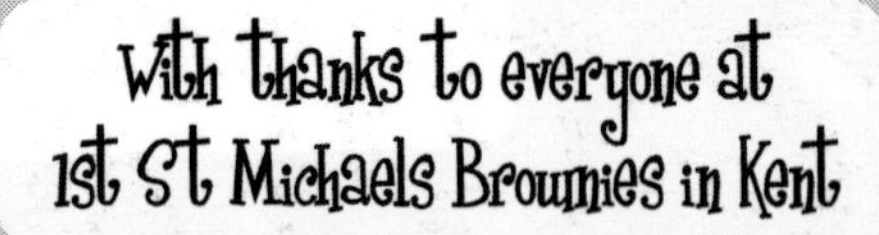

STRIPES PUBLISHING
An imprint of Magi Publications
1 The Coda Centre, 189 Munster Road,
London SW6 6AW

A paperback original. First published in Great Britain in 2009
Published by arrangement with Girlguiding UK.

ISBN: 978-1-84715-101-8

A CIP catalogue record for this book is available from the British Library.

Printed and bound in the UK.
2 4 6 8 10 9 7 5 3 1

Brownies

Perfect Promise

stripes

Meet the Brownies

Katie

Katie, Grace's twin, is super sporty and likes to play games and win. She wants to get every Brownie badge and her Six is Foxes!

Jamila

Jamila's got too many brothers, so she loves Brownies because NO BOYS ARE ALLOWED! Jamila is a Badger!

Ellie

Awesome
at art and crafts,
Ellie used to be a
Rainbow and likes
making new friends.
Ellie is a Hedgehog!

Animal-crazy
Charlie has a guinea
pig called Nibbles. She
loves Brownie quizzes
and Pow Wows. Her
Six is Squirrels!

Charlie

Grace

Grace
is Katie's twin
sister and she's
ballet bonkers.
Grace enjoys going
on Brownie outings,
and she is a
Rabbit!

Chapter 1

It was a sunny Tuesday lunchtime and all the children at Badenbridge Primary School were in the playground. Over in the corner, on a bench underneath a tree, sat five best friends.

"I can't wait for tonight!" said Katie. "We're finally going to be Brownies!"

"At last," sighed her twin sister Grace as she twiddled her long blonde hair in her fingers. "It feels like we've waited for ages."

"That's because we have," Jamila pointed out, tucking her long dark hair behind her ears. "We put our names down on the 'waiting to join' list months ago."

"It was so lucky that my mum found out

about Brownies before we moved here!" said Ellie. Ellie had only just moved to Badenbridge, but it hadn't taken her long to meet her new friends Katie, Grace, Jamila and Charlie.

Charlie smiled at Ellie. "Yes, because now you can join with us!"

"Mum says we'll do loads of exciting stuff at Brownies," said Katie. "Games, adventure days and all kinds of outings."

"And crafts and cookery," added Ellie.

"And there are NO BOYS!" Jamila smiled. "That is just going to be so good!"

The others laughed. Jamila had four older brothers and got fed up being the only girl.

"Exactly," said Charlie, whose brown hair was tied up in bunches. "Boo says Brownies

is great." Boo was Charlie's big sister, and she'd been a Brownie for two years. "She's been on outings – like to the pantomime, and concerts, even to the zoo."

"We might get to put on a show," said Grace, who loved to dance and did ballet and jazz classes every week. "And you might be able to do your music, Jamila!"

Just like Grace loved to dance, Jamila loved to make music. She played the keyboard in a music group on Saturdays.

"Like I said," giggled Katie, "I can't wait for tonight!"

"Because we all want to be Brownies!" the five girls yelled together. They all laughed.

"What do you think we should wear?" asked Grace. "Do you think we need to wear our school uniforms?"

"Er, no thanks!" said Katie, pulling a face.

"Who'd wear that when they don't absolutely have to?"

"Not me!" agreed Jamila. "But I haven't got my Brownie clothes yet. Mum says I've got to see if I like Brownies before she'll buy them for me."

"What's not to like about Brownies?" Charlie said. "There's going to be loads of things to like!"

Jamila giggled. "I know! I tried to tell her that. I'm hoping she'll take me shopping on Saturday."

"We looked on the Brownie website," said Grace. "Mum's ordered our outfits on it. I really like the yellow waistcoat thing that you put your badges on. And the skort!"

"A skort?" said Ellie. "What's that?"

"It's like a pair of shorts, but it has a piece of material across the front which makes it

look like a skirt," explained Grace. "It'll be great for running around in."

"I like the hoodie!" stated Katie. "It'll be really good to wear with the leggings so I can do lots of sports stuff. I'm going in jeans tonight because of all the games and activities we'll do." Katie was a serious sports fan.

"I'm going to wear my old Rainbows uniform," said Ellie. "It just about still fits!"

Ellie had been a Rainbow before she'd moved to Badenbridge with her mum. It had been brilliant fun, but now she couldn't wait to join Brownies!

"I've already got some of my cousin's Brownie clothes," said Charlie. "She's moved up to Guides now and she gave me her old T-shirts and hoodie. Mum and Dad said they'll take me to get the trousers soon."

Suddenly, she felt a sharp tap on her shoulder.

"BOO!"

Charlie and her friends jumped with surprise.

"What?" she shrieked, as she turned round. "Oh – it's you!"

The "BOO!" had come from Boo, her sister, who was standing right behind her.

"So you're all coming to Brownies tonight then?" Boo grinned.

"Yes," said Jamila excitedly. "What do we do when we first get there? Do you think the Brownie Leaders will know we're coming?"

“Of course!” said Boo. “Vicky rang your parents, didn’t she? So she’ll be expecting you. And she should have sent you a Brownie Welcome Card – didn’t you all get one?”

“Oh yes!” all the friends confirmed.

“So what are you worried about then?” wondered Boo.

“Who’s Vicky?” asked Ellie.

“She’s the lady who runs Brownies,” said Boo. “She’s helped by another lady called Sam. They’re really good fun.”

Grace smiled with relief. She was feeling a bit nervous about what to expect at Brownies that night. She and Katie didn’t have any older sisters who were Brownies – only a mum who had been a Brownie ages ago, and Grace was certain that Brownies must be totally different now after such a long, long time.

"You'll be fine," laughed Boo. "Everyone at Brownies is great. You'll love it."

"Oooh." Grace hugged herself and smiled. "I really, really can't wait for tonight!"

The 1st Badenbridge Brownie unit met every Tuesday evening in the school hall.

Ellie's mum was working late that night, so Ellie had gone home with Katie and Grace. At five o'clock, their mum took the three friends to Brownies together. Jamila arrived with her gran, and Charlie cycled there with her dad and Boo.

"Well, hello," smiled a friendly lady in jeans. She had a smart blue sweatshirt with some important-looking badges on it. One of them said VICKY, BROWNIE LEADER.

"You must be our new Brownies," said Vicky. "Now," she looked at her clipboard and ran her finger down a list of names. "I should have Jamila, Charlie, Ellie, Katie and Grace."

"I recognize Charlie. You've already been here lots of times to collect Boo, haven't you?" Vicky smiled kindly and Charlie grinned and nodded back. "Now the rest of you – who is who?"

The girls nervously said their names.

"Excellent," said Vicky. "You know, we haven't had any twins in our unit for ages!" She smiled at Katie and Grace. "It's a good job you've got different hairstyles or I might get myself confused! Now, we've already started a game, so why don't you all go and join in?" Vicky pointed over to the other Brownies, who were throwing beanbags to one another and giggling. Whatever game they were playing, it looked fun! "I'll be taking the register in a minute and then I'll introduce you to each of your Sixers. See you in a bit!"

"What's a Sixer?" Jamila wanted to know.

"The Sixers are in charge of the Sixes!" said Ellie, who'd heard about Brownies when she'd been at Rainbows.

"What's a Six?" whispered Grace, feeling a little anxious as they walked over to join the other Brownies.

"They're the groups that make up a Brownie unit," said Ellie.

"What?" gasped Katie with a look of surprise. "You mean that we might not all be in the same group...?"

Chapter 2

After taking the register, Vicky introduced the five new Brownies to the unit. They all felt especially important when the others gave them a clap to welcome them.

"I won't tell you the names of the rest of the Brownies," she said to the girls. "There's too many of them, but you'll get to know everyone soon. And I'm sure that some of you know each other already from school. But I will introduce you to Sam, our other Brownie Leader."

"Hello, girls," grinned Sam, who also looked

smart in her blue fleece. She handed Vicky a list. "I hope you'll be very happy at Brownies."

"And this is Daisy," said Vicky, pointing out a girl who was dressed in a Guide outfit. "Daisy used to be a Brownie with us, but she's now a Guide. She comes to help us out as a Young Leader. Oh – and she's my daughter, too!"

Daisy smiled and waved.

"Now," said Vicky. "Could I ask our Sixers to come here, please?"

Five older Brownies walked over to Vicky. All of them had Brownie sashes or Brownie gilets covered in badges.

"So, Jamila, you're with Izzy in Badgers," said Vicky, consulting her list. "Charlie you're joining Squirrels and this is your Sixer, Megan. It's Rabbits for Grace, so you go off with

Molly, and Katie you're to go with Jessica and join the Foxes. That leaves Lauren and the Hedgehogs, who'd like Ellie to join them! Right, girls! Sixers, can you introduce our new Brownies to your Sixes, please?"

Ellie, Katie, Grace, Jamila and Charlie looked at each other. Jamila smiled weakly at her friends and said, "See you later," before she went over to join her Six.

The five best friends *were* being split up!

Ellie's Sixer, Lauren, introduced her to the rest of the Six.

"This is Ellie and she's joining Hedgehogs. And this is Amy, Sukia and Poppy!"

"Hey, Ellie!" The three girls smiled at her.

"And I'm going to be your Brownie Buddy!" said Poppy.

"What's that?" asked Ellie.

"I'm going to help you out in your first few weeks at Brownies," Poppy explained. "Just ask if you don't understand anything."

"Thanks!" Ellie grinned.

"We're making bookmarks tonight," added Amy, who was wearing a badge that said "Seconder" on it. She explained that the Seconder helped the Sixer to run the Six. "We're designing the bookmarks for a nature project we've

all been working on. They've got to have pictures of animals or nature stuff on them. You can do one too!"

Ellie smiled. She loved everything to do with art and crafts.

There was a box on the table full of colouring pens, paper, card and scissors for the Six to share. Soon Ellie was busy designing her own bookmark, and chatting away with her Six.

Over on the Squirrels table, Megan and the Seconder Ashvini had introduced Charlie to her Six too.

"Bethany!" she exclaimed when she spotted one girl.

"Hi, Charlie!" Bethany said. "I didn't know you were joining Brownies!"

Charlie giggled. "And I didn't know you

were already a Brownie!"

Bethany also went to Badenbridge Primary, although the girls were in different classes. The other girl in the Squirrels was called Faith and she was really friendly too.

"Looks like Bethany should be your Brownie Buddy!" said Megan.

"Cool!" said Bethany. "Come on, I'll explain all about that later – but right now we've got to get on with our bookmarks. All the Sixes are making them. We might even get a Brownie sticker if we do a good job!"

The Rabbits, Foxes and Badgers were all busy with their bookmarks too. Grace, Katie and Jamila had quickly made friends with their Sixes and been introduced to their Brownie Buddies. Grace had discovered that Boo was her Seconder, and that another of the Rabbits, Caitlin, was her friend from ballet class! Over in the Hedgehogs, Ellie realized that Poppy already knew Jamila from their music class. And Katie's Sixer in Foxes was Jessica from her swimming class. There were lots of other girls from the school drama club too! It seemed like everyone who was fun was a Brownie!

Daisy went round the hall helping all the Sixes with their bookmarks. So did Vicky and Sam, who explained to the new girls that the bookmarks were part of a project they were doing with the Badenbridge Nature Centre, which was due to open next month. The mother of Amber, one of the Brownies, worked at the centre and she'd asked if they'd like to help out with setting up all the children's activities.

Jamila, Ellie, Katie, Grace and Charlie had heard about the centre – it was exciting to be part of something so new! To link in with the

Nature Centre, Vicky and Sam explained that some of the Brownies were working on a badge called Wildlife explorer. Others were hoping to get their Environment badge.

After a while, Vicky called everyone together and said that it was time for their Pow Wow.

"What's a Pow Wow?" Katie asked Jessica.

"It's a special kind of Brownie meeting. We don't have one every time we're at Brownies though," grinned Jessica. "Don't worry, you'll soon get to know what's going on!"

"Come on," urged Emma, the Foxes Seconder. "We've got to get ready!"

Vicky and Sam sat on chairs in the middle of the hall and all the Brownies gathered together in a circle on the floor in front of them.

"We have to stay in our Six," Izzy, the Sixer of Badgers explained to Jamila.

"Pow Wows are when Vicky tells us about things Brownies are doing all over the country – everywhere in the world sometimes!" said Holly.

"And Pow Wows are when we get the chance to decide what we want to do at Brownies too!" said Jasmine, sitting down next to Jamila.

Just then, Vicky and Sam put up their right hands. All the

other Brownies stopped chatting and did the same, so the five best friends did too.

"Thank you, girls," said Sam. "Now, who's got news this week?"

Everyone listened as some of the Brownies told the unit about things they'd done at school or other clubs they went to. One of the girls in Badgers announced that her mum was going to have a baby. Then Vicky and Sam talked to the Brownies about the Nature Centre.

"I know that some of you are working on Brownie badges that are linked with the centre," said Sam, "so you might be pleased to know that we're all going there for a Brownie outing soon!"

Everyone cheered with excitement.

"Please, Sam!" said lots of the Brownies at once. "What kind of outing?"

"Well, there will be a fun nature trail to try out and perhaps some other things too," said Sam mysteriously. "We'll have letters for you to take home about it next week."

"In the meantime, I think you're all doing a brilliant job on your bookmarks," said Vicky.

"Yes," agreed Sam. "I don't think we've ever had so many creative girls at First Badenbridge Brownies before!"

"Remember, there's no race to finish," said Vicky. "You'll have time to do a bit more on

them later. The Nature Centre wants to put all the bookmarks on display when it opens!"

The Brownies exchanged excited glances.

"OK, girls," Sam said. "What would you like to do now? A song or a game?"

"A SONG!" yelled some of the Brownies.

"A GAME!" screamed the others.

Vicky and Sam laughed. "How about a song first and a game later?" Vicky suggested.

All the girls cheered.

Chapter 3

Katie, Grace, Jamila, Ellie and Charlie just loved the singing. They didn't know the words to the first song, but they soon picked up the chorus. The second song was one they knew from school, so there was no problem singing that at the top of their voices!

Afterwards, the Brownies sang a song that they had to mime to. The five best friends hadn't a clue what the words or the actions were and made tons of mistakes. But the more they got it wrong, the funnier it seemed to be, and soon they were laughing so much they couldn't sing!

After singing, it was time to do a bit more work on their bookmarks. The girls didn't have a chance to catch up with each other until afterwards, when they stopped to help themselves to a glass of water from a jug that had been put out on a side table.

"I am SO thirsty," gasped Charlie.

"Me too!" said Ellie.

"I nearly fell over in that last song," giggled Jamila. "I wobbled so much when we had to lift our leg up!"

"Are you all enjoying your first Brownie meeting?" asked Daisy, coming over to join them.

"You bet!" exclaimed Ellie, flicking back her long red plaits. "It's like Rainbows but even better!"

"I can't believe how much stuff we've done," said Charlie.

"So you think you'll all be back next week then?" Daisy asked, smiling.

"Definitely!" said Jamila.

"Just try and stop us!" agreed Katie.

"I wonder what we'll do next?" Ellie asked.

But before any of her friends could answer, Ellie realized that the room was falling silent. Vicky and Sam were holding up their right hands again.

"Thank you, Brownies," Vicky said when everyone was standing still and quiet. "Now, I think you all wanted to play a game!"

"Yay!"

The room was filled with noise again as all the Brownies raced to stand in front of Vicky.

"How about Traffic Lights," Vicky suggested.

There was more cheering from the happy Brownies. Traffic Lights was obviously a brilliant game, the five new Brownies thought, as they listened to the instructions. First, everyone had to line up in a long, straight line in front of Vicky. When Sam called out "RED", "AMBER" or "GREEN", the

Brownies had to run to different parts of the hall. If you were the last person to reach a light, or you went to the wrong one, you were out. It sounded easy but it was really hard, especially when everyone got the giggles.

Sometimes, Sam caught them out by calling out the light that everyone was already standing at! Traffic Lights was great fun and they played it three times.

At the end of the third game, Vicky put up her right hand again. The giggling Brownies all did the same and fell silent.

"OK, girls," said Sam. "If you'd like to get your things together and bring them into the Brownie Ring, it's time for us to get ready to go home."

"Already?" sighed Ellie.

"But I want to stay and do it all again!" exclaimed Charlie.

The Brownies gathered round in a circle, just like they had earlier.

"Now, whose turn is it to read our Thought for the Week?" Sam asked.

Daisy glanced at a piece of paper she was holding.

"Ashvini!" she said.

"OK then," said Sam. "Ashvini – what have you written for us to think about?"

Ashvini smiled and opened an important-looking book. Then she said, "We are glad to be Brownies and to have so many Brownie friends. This week all the First Badenbridge Brownies will try to remember to be helpful and kind to everyone we live with and everyone we meet."

"Thank you, Ashvini," said Vicky. "That was fantastic. And I think it's given us something to think about over the next week, hasn't it?"

"I'm sure that all of us will remember to help someone out this week. And we'll all keep smiling, won't we?" agreed Sam.

All the Brownies nodded, grinning.

Then Vicky presented Jamila, Charlie, Ellie, Katie and Grace with their own special booklet.

"This is to welcome each of you to the First Badenbridge Brownies," Vicky said. "It'll tell you all about becoming a Brownie, and it will also help you to get ready for your Promise Celebration."

The five best friends looked at each other and smiled. They couldn't wait to look inside the booklet!

"I'm also going to give you these," Sam said, handing each of the five girls a leaflet. "This is for you to give to the adult who is collecting you tonight. It tells them all about Brownies and the things that you'll get up to while you are here."

"Now, girls," said Vicky, "it's time for us to say goodnight."

All the Brownies in the Ring held hands and sang:

Time for the end,
Our meeting's passed.
Brownies is great,
Time flies so fast!

After the meeting, the five friends gathered outside with their parents, who had come to take them home.

"That was just the best!" said Katie.

"I can't wait until next week!" agreed Jamila.

"Or to read our new booklet!" said Charlie.

"There was so much fun stuff to do!" exclaimed Grace.

"I want it to be Brownies every day!" sighed Ellie.

And then the tired new Brownies went home.

Chapter 4

At school the next day, the five friends couldn't wait till breaktime to talk about everything they'd got up to at Brownies.

"I read that booklet Vicky gave us in bed last night," said Charlie.

"So did I!" said Grace. "And I started to fill in all the stuff about me – there's a place to put in your name and your Six."

"I haven't started that yet," sighed Katie. "I was reading the story which explains what being a Brownie is all about. It was really good."

"Brownies is such great fun," said Jamila. "And Chloe, my Brownie Buddy, was ever so nice. But then so were all the other girls!"

Ellie nodded in agreement, but she had a worried look on her face.

"What's up, Ellie?" asked Jamila. "Wasn't Poppy great too?"

"Oh yes, she was really nice," said Ellie. "But I can't help thinking it's a shame that you couldn't all be in Hedgehogs with me."

"What's so special about Hedgehogs?" asked Katie.

"Nothing," said Ellie. "It would just have been good if we'd all been in the same Six."

"It would," Grace agreed. "Although one of the really good things about Brownies is that we've already made lots of new friends."

"And we've still got each other for the rest of the time as well as at Brownies!" declared Charlie.

"Well, if we had all been in the same Six,"

Katie said, "it would have been best if it had been Foxes."

"Why?" Jamila asked, looking puzzled.

"Because Foxes are the best," stated Katie.

"What makes you say that?" Ellie replied.

"Well, it's obvious," Katie pointed out. "The Foxes won two games of Traffic Lights last night. And I looked at everyone else's bookmarks and ours are definitely the nicest."

"That's not true!" Charlie exclaimed. "All the Sixes are good."

"Yes," agreed Grace. "Just because Foxes won some of the games last night doesn't mean they always do!"

"Well, they were the best last night!" Katie said crossly.

"Perhaps they were just lucky," Ellie said.

"Or perhaps they're just show-offs!" snapped Grace. "That's typical of you, Katie!

Why do you always have to be the first or the best or the cleverest?"

"What's wrong with that?" Katie huffed. "Mum says it's good when I win swimming races!"

Katie loved all sport but she was especially good at swimming. She always tried hard to win races.

"There's nothing wrong with being good at stuff," Jamila said, trying to calm the sisters down. "It's just that all the Sixes at Brownies are good."

"And remember what that girl Ashvini said at the end of Brownies?" mentioned Charlie. "We have to be kind to one another."

The five friends looked at each other.

"OK, OK," said Katie. "Sorry, Grace. Rabbits are just as good. And so are the Badgers, Hedgehogs and Squirrels."

Her four friends smiled at her.

"But don't forget, you'll have to try hard to beat the Foxes next week!" Katie grinned.

"Aaargh!" The others all laughed.

"Oh – and don't forget you're all coming to mine for tea tomorrow too!" giggled Ellie.

The next day after school, the five best friends were all sitting in Ellie's bedroom. It was the day that her mum came home from work early so she often let Ellie have her friends round. On other days, Ellie went to an after-school club until her mum could pick her up.

Charlie rummaged in her school bag and pulled out a large book. "Look what Boo gave me as we were leaving school. It's her copy of the *Brownie Badge Book*."

"Fantastic!" said Katie, peering eagerly over Charlie's shoulder. "I want to see what it says about those badges Vicky and Sam were talking about on Tuesday."

"You mean the Explorer badge?" said Grace.

"I think it was called Wildlife explorer," said Jamila. "And there was an Environment badge too."

"What do you think you have to do for that?" wondered Ellie.

"Ummm," Charlie muttered, as she flicked through the book. "It's about recycling and endangered species – excellent!"

"And what does it say about the Wildlife one?" asked Grace.

Charlie turned the pages of the book again. "Cool!" she exclaimed. "It's all about animals! Finding out their names and feeding wildlife – how great is that! Look."

She handed the book to Katie, who pored eagerly through the pages.

"They all sound good to me," she said. "I'd like to do every one of them!"

“Look!” said Charlie, pointing at one of the pages. “There’s even a Friend to animals badge.”

Charlie loved animals, especially her guinea pig, Nibbles. She wanted to be a vet when she was older.

The girls turned the pages of Boo’s book and found lots of things that interested them. Jamila liked the idea of working for her Musician badge and Grace couldn’t wait to start her Dancer badge. Katie fancied the idea of doing the Sports badge.

“What badge would you like to do, Ellie?” asked Jamila.

“Maybe the Craft badge,” Ellie replied. “But I’d like to do the Artist badge too!”

"Vicky did say that we have to make our Brownie Promise before we can start any badges properly," Grace pointed out.

"I'm dreading that already!" sighed Charlie. "I started to learn it from the booklet Vicky gave us, but it's hard – I just can't remember it!"

"Well, we won't have our Promise Celebration for a few weeks," said Ellie. "You've got loads of time to learn it."

"And we'll help you!" said Jamila. "We can all learn it together. Come on!"

The Brownie Promise was made by all girls who wanted to be Brownies and they had to say their Promise out loud at their Celebration. Whenever a Brownie said her Promise, she held her hand up in a special way. It was called the Brownie Sign.

The five best friends raised their right hand

at their sides and folded down their little finger and thumb just like they'd seen the other Brownies do in the Ring.

"I promise that I will do my best..." they began and then Charlie put her hand over her mouth in horror.

"You see," she declared. "I can't even remember the second line! Oh dear! I'll never become a Brownie!"

Chapter 5

The next morning, Jamila hurried into school, eager to find Charlie. "Hey, Charlie, this is for you!" she said, handing over a large piece of paper with some writing on it.

"What is it?" Charlie asked.

"It's the Brownie Promise." Jamila grinned. "I did it for you in great big writing on the computer. I thought you could stick it on your bedroom wall and then it might be easier to learn."

"Thanks!" said Charlie, giving her friend a hug. "That's a great idea! You're being helpful and kind just like our Brownie Thought for the Week said we should be!"

"You're welcome!" Jamila replied. "And we can keep on learning the Promise and Brownie Law together at lunchtime too."

Just then, Katie and Grace arrived.

"Hey, guess what!" Katie butted in. "Our Brownie outfits arrived in the post!"

"Cool!" said Charlie.

"What clothes did you get?" asked Ellie, who had just joined them.

"I've got the hoodie and a T-shirt,"

declared Katie. "Plus some cool leggings, a sash – to put zillions of badges on, of course! – and a baseball cap."

"Wow!" said Ellie, feeling envious. "How about you, Grace?"

"Um, I chose the skort, a gilet and a T-shirt," she said. "I'm going to sew my badges on to the gilet."

"What's a gilet?" asked Jamila.

"It's that waistcoat thing," explained Grace.

"You're so lucky," said Jamila. "I'm going with Mum to get mine tomorrow but my stupid brothers are coming too. They're bound to muck about while we're there."

According to Jamila, her four brothers were loud and messy and always making fun of her. Sometimes, the only place she could be anywhere without boys was in her bedroom. But now she had another place – Brownies!

"I'm going to the shops tomorrow too," said Charlie. "Dad's going to get me some trousers to go with the hoodie and T-shirts my cousin gave me."

"My mum can't take me to get my Brownie clothes until next week!" sighed Ellie. "So I'll still be in my Rainbow ones – I'll be the only one..."

Jamila put her arm round Ellie.

"Don't worry," she said to her friend. "You'll get your clothes soon."

The bell rang for the start of school and they made their way indoors.

The rest of the day went by in a flash and soon it was the weekend. On Saturday, the best friends were all invited to the birthday party of one of the girls in their class, Natalie. It was at a place called Crocodiles, which was a giant indoor play area filled with climbing frames, ball ponds that you could roll around in, and trampolines. The party was really good fun, and it was one of the only times that the five friends didn't talk about Brownies! But they still behaved like Brownies by helping Natalie's mum hand out the party bags.

On Sunday, Katie took part in a swimming gala. All the others went along to cheer her on. The last race came down to a sprint finish and Katie won by a whisker! At last, though, it was Tuesday again – Brownie night!

"Hello, girls," smiled Sam, as she saw them arrive. "My goodness – don't you look smart in your new Brownie clothes?"

Katie, Grace, Jamila and Charlie all had their new Brownie kit on, and grinned with pride. But Ellie just looked sad.

"I promise I'll have my new clothes next week," she said.

"That's not a problem, Ellie!" Sam said kindly. "Now off you go to your Sixes and get yourselves busy finishing off your bookmarks."

Ellie rushed over to the Hedgehogs, eager to get on. Lauren and Amy were already there, getting everything ready for the others so Ellie asked if she could help. She was just putting some colouring pens on the table when Daisy came over.

"Hey, is that your bookmark?" she asked Ellie. "It's fantastic!"

"Thanks," said Ellie, beaming.

After thinking about the nature theme they were following, she'd used the names of all the Brownie Sixes to create her bookmark design. She was really pleased with it and thrilled that Daisy thought it was good too.

The hall was filled with the noise of friendly chatter and laughter as more and more Brownies arrived and got busy with their bookmarks. Most of them had nearly finished when Vicky called everyone to the Brownie Ring.

The Brownies all sat down and waited. Vicky looked round and smiled. "Some of you are working towards exciting new badges, so I thought perhaps those Brownies could stand up and tell the others what you are doing. So … who's doing their Wildlife explorer badge?"

Several hands shot up.

"Caitlin! Perhaps you could tell everyone what that involves?" asked Vicky.

Caitlin, one of the Rabbits, stood up.

"Well, one of the things you can do is spend fifteen minutes a day watching birds,"

she said, fiddling with her sash. "I've been going to my gran's every day this week after school and watching the birds in her garden. She's got a feeding table and loads of them come to visit. Gran's got this bird book and she helps me to work out what sort of birds they are. I've written them all down in a notebook and I've got to try and learn some of their names for when I get tested. Oh – and I put food out as well. Gran's taught me how to make a kind of bird cake thing out of nuts, seeds and raisins.

It's really gross, but the birds love it!"

All the Brownies giggled.

"Sounds like you've been really busy," Sam said. "Is there anything else you've got to do before you present your project?"

"I've still got to build a feeding station," Caitlin declared. "Dad's going to help me make one for hedgehogs next weekend."

"Well done," Vicky said. "And perhaps Poppy can tell us about her Environment badge?"

Poppy shot straight up and told everyone about how she'd been collecting packaging such as milk cartons and cornflake packets so that it could be recycled instead of thrown away. She'd also been finding out about where some of the food in the supermarket had come from and how far it had had to travel.

"I've got to find out about how the things we do use energy," Poppy finished. "Like leaving the lights on, or the TV on standby."

"What a busy bunch of Brownies you all are," Vicky said. "Not everyone likes to do badges, but if any of you aren't doing any at the moment and you'd like to, come and talk to either me or Sam or your Sixer."

"Now – our outing," Sam said.

All the Brownies sat up excitedly.

"We're going to the new Badenbridge Nature Centre in two weeks' time," Sam

explained. "You'll remember that Amber's mum works there, and that we've been asked to test out some of the children's activities for them?"

Holly shot up her hand.

"And please, Vicky! We're doing our bookmarks so that they can be put on display at the Nature Centre too!" she said.

"We are, Holly – thank you!" said Vicky. "So, we'll walk to the Nature Centre because it's only ten minutes away from here and we'll be doing a scavenger hunt on the way! And when we get there, we'll do the nature trail that the centre would like us to try out."

Katie put up her hand. "What's a scavenger hunt?"

"It's a bit like a treasure hunt. You get given a list of things to look out for and identify," Vicky explained. "When you spot them, you tick them off your list. Usually, you'd be asked to collect the items, but some of the things on the list would be difficult to carry away with you – you'll see what I mean on the day!"

The Brownies looked at each other, curious as to what Vicky meant.

"I've got a letter for you to take home about it," she continued. "Make sure you get permission from a parent or carer to come on the hunt and bring the signed form with you next week."

Jamila, Katie, Grace, Ellie and Charlie exchanged excited glances. Their first Brownie outing – already!

"Now," said Sam, "shall we play a game?"

"Yes!" shouted all the Brownies.

Chapter 6

The next day, the five best friends were sitting in the garden at Katie and Grace's house after school.

"Hey!" said Grace. "Did we tell you we're going to put up a bird table? Dad's going to help us make it at the weekend."

"That sounds like fun," said Jamila.

"Are you going to do your Wildlife explorer badge?" asked Charlie.

"We thought we'd speak to Vicky about it and ask if we can count it towards the badge once we've done our Promise," Katie explained. "I really hope she says we can!"

"And we're hoping we might be able to feed some hedgehogs as well," Grace said.

"Wow," exclaimed Ellie. "You're so lucky. We haven't even got a balcony in our flat."

"Well, you can come and see it whenever you like," said Katie. "All of you can. In fact, why don't you come over on Sunday?"

"Yes," said Grace, "we can watch the birds together!"

"Cool!" said Charlie.

On Friday morning, Ellie arrived at school looking fed up.

"What's the matter?" Jamila asked.

"I was meant to go with Mum last night to get my Brownie outfit and then she got this phone call to say she had to go back to work!" said Ellie.

"So you didn't get it?" Jamila wondered.

"No," Ellie sighed. "And I had to go into work with Mum and sit in her boring old office while she spent absolutely ages doing something on her computer. It's so not fair!"

Grace smiled at her friend. "But you'll be able to get it at the weekend, won't you?"

"I hope so," Ellie replied. "It's just that I was so looking forward to getting it."

"And now you can look forward to it all over again!" said Charlie, and the girls laughed.

"How are you doing with learning your Brownie Promise, Charlie?" asked Jamila.

"Hmmm," said Charlie. "Sometimes it's OK … but other times, I can't remember a word!"

"Come on then!" said Grace. "Let's all say it together now!"

On Saturday, Katie and Grace spent ages with their dad making the bird table and choosing the best place to put it.

"If we have it right next to the fence, then cats could reach it too," Grace pointed out.

"Same if it's too near a tree," Katie agreed.

In the end, they managed to find a safe place that they could still see from the house. They added a special bird feeder to it – one that the lady in the garden centre said would let birds feed, but that squirrels couldn't steal the food from. They had bought some bird food at the same time, and the lady told them they should look at the website for the RSPB to see what else the birds in their garden might like to eat.

"What's the RSPB?" Katie had asked.

"It stands for the Royal Society for the Protection of Birds," her dad had explained. "We can look up their site at home."

As soon as they'd set up the table and feeder, Katie, Grace and their dad sat in the living room at the computer. They had a great view of the garden from the window.

"It says we shouldn't feed the birds milk," said Katie, "or they'll get tummy ache."

"But we can give them grated cheddar," Grace read. "And they love unsalted peanuts and black sunflower seeds."

"Well," Dad said, "it sounds as if we need to make ourselves a bird food shopping list!"

"And we should ask Caitlin for her gran's bird cake recipe," said Katie.

"Look!" Grace whispered. "On the bird table – it's a little bird!"

"Oh, it's a robin!" said Dad. "Can you see it looks like it's wearing a red T-shirt?"

"And there's another one!" said Grace.

"They're so sweet," sighed Katie. "I really wish we'd already made our Promise – then we could get our Wildlife explorer badge even sooner!"

Ellie, Jamila and Charlie came round to see the bird table on Sunday.

"We've counted ten birds so far," said Katie.

"But four of them have been robins," said Grace, "so it might be the same two robins that keep coming back!"

"They sound like greedy robins to me," said Charlie, smiling.

The others giggled. The girls sat for a while to see if any other birds came to the table, but there were no more visitors.

"Shall we go up to our room?" suggested Grace. "We can check on the table later."

Grace and Katie shared a bedroom and had beds on opposite sides of the room. On Grace's side, the walls were covered in posters of ballerinas and certificates for ballet

and jazz dance exams. On Katie's side, she'd hung up all her medals that she'd won for swimming competitions, as well as pictures she'd cut out of magazines and newspapers of some of her favourite sporting heroes. It was almost as if their bedroom was two rooms in one!

"I got my Brownie clothes yesterday!" Ellie told her friends excitedly.

"That's brilliant, Ellie." Jamila smiled.

"Now we'll all be in our Brownie outfits on Tuesday!" said Katie.

"I can't believe we've been Brownies for less than two weeks," said Jamila. "We've done so many new things already!"

"And we're going to the Nature Centre soon," said Ellie. "I can't wait to do the nature trail. And the scavenger hunt!"

"Hey, why don't we do a scavenger hunt in the garden," said Katie. "We can have two teams, and each think up a list of things for the other team to find."

The others cheered excitedly.

"That's a great idea," said Charlie.

"Let's get started straight away," said Jamila.

And that's exactly what they did!

An hour later, the girls were sitting on the grass in the garden, having a refreshing snack of juice and biscuits.

"That was brilliant," said Grace, "even though we didn't get ten out of ten."

"Yes," said Ellie. "How were me and Grace supposed to spot a robin in the garden with the five of us tearing around? We'd have terrified any birds!"

"Well, you had us searching for a four-leafed clover, which was just as impossible," giggled Jamila.

"But we did find thousands of three-leafed ones," said Charlie, laughing. "That was such fun."

"And we wouldn't have had the idea if it hadn't been for Brownies," Katie pointed out.

Ellie sighed. "I can't wait for Tuesday."

"Nor me," the others all said at once.

In no time at all it was Tuesday again, but as soon as Katie and Grace arrived at school it was obvious they'd had a big row.

"What's up?" Charlie asked.

"It's her!" Katie said, pointing at her twin sister. "She started it."

"Started what?" Jamila asked.

"I did not!" Grace declared. "You never give me a chance with the bird table. Every time I try to put food out, you've already done it. You did it on Sunday and then you did it again yesterday!"

"Well, it's not my fault if you don't think of feeding the birds first before you eat your own breakfast!" Katie shouted.

"Aaagh!" Grace yelled back. "You always have to be first!"

Charlie, Ellie and Jamila tried to calm the two sisters down, but whatever anyone said, neither Katie nor Grace would say sorry.

"This is crazy," Jamila said. "I thought you two were doing this project together?"

The sisters didn't reply. They turned their backs on one another and refused to speak. And they didn't seem to want to speak to Jamila, Ellie or Charlie either.

Katie and Grace still weren't speaking to each other at lunchtime. "Look," Jamila said, "this is silly! You both want to do the bird table, don't you?"

Grace and Katie said nothing, but nodded their heads.

"OK, I've got an idea – so that you can share it."

"Share it?" Katie said, puzzled. "How can we do that – split it in half?"

Charlie and Ellie giggled. Grace just looked even more puzzled than Katie.

"Easy," Jamila said. "Come up with a timetable or a calendar or something..."

"Oh – you mean a rota!" Charlie said. "It tells you who's doing what and when."

Katie and Grace still looked puzzled.

"Exactly," said Jamila. "You make a chart that has the days of the week on it and then you each put your names down for some of the days. So Katie tops up the bird feed on Monday and Grace does it on Tuesday. Then Katie does it again on Wednesday, and so on."

"Hey, that's a great idea." Grace smiled.

Jamila was so clever at sorting things out!

"It's brilliant," said Ellie. "So are you two going to give it a try?"

Katie shrugged her shoulders, but didn't say anything.

"I will," said Grace. "If Katie will make up with me. I'm sorry, Katie. I didn't mean to say horrid things to you."

Katie looked at her sister. Slowly a smile appeared on her face.

"Nor me. I'm sorry too."

And the two sisters hugged and made up.

Chapter 7

That night, the five best friends met up at the hall and settled into their Sixes. All the Brownies had finished their bookmarks at the last meeting, and Vicky and Sam had collected them to give to the Nature Centre.

"Now," said Vicky, "we've got a wordsearch for you all to do tonight. Actually, there are two – you can choose which one you want to do. One has animal words and the other one is about the environment. Sam and I will come round and see how you're getting on."

Over at the Foxes, Daisy was handing out the different sheets.

"Can I have the animal one, please?" Katie asked. Straight away, she found the word ROBIN. But there were lots more words to find and some of them looked impossibly hard.

"Which words have you found?" Emma, the Seconder of Foxes, asked her. "I've got SPARROW and look, they were really sneaky and put it sideways *and* backwards!"

"I've found BLACKBIRD!" Katie said and soon the girls were huddled together helping each other find the rest.

All around the hall, the Brownies worked away and finished off their wordsearches. Then Sam announced they were going to play a game. But just as they were about to start, Vicky called Ellie, Grace, Charlie, Jamila and Katie over to see her.

"I've called a special little Pow Wow for you to talk about your Promise Celebrations."

The five best friends exchanged glances. What was Vicky going to tell them?

"The Promise Celebration is a very important and exciting time for every Brownie," said Vicky.

She explained to them that when they made the Brownie Promise they were pledging to do their best to follow the three parts of the Promise.

"Is that to love our God?" asked Jamila.

Vicky nodded.

"And to serve the Queen and the country?" asked Ellie.

"Yes!" Vicky said.

"And to help other people and keep the Brownie Guide Law!" said Katie.

"Well done, girls!" laughed Vicky. "Can any of you remember what the Brownie Law is?"

"Umm," said Grace. "Is it doing a good turn every day?"

"Oh – and thinking of others before myself!" added Katie with her hand up.

"Yes!" said Vicky. "I can see you are all going to make wonderful Brownies!"

The five Brownies grinned at their Leader.

"It's up to you girls to decide how you celebrate your Promise," Vicky explained. "You'll be ready to have your Celebrations in a couple of weeks. Have you any ideas about what you'd like to do?"

"You mean we can choose what kind of Celebration we have?" asked Katie.

"Yes," said Vicky.

"My friend where I used to live had her Promise Celebration at the swimming pool!" explained Ellie.

"Wow!" exclaimed the others.

"Can our families come?" asked Grace.

"Of course," said Vicky. "They can come and be part of it and take photos too."

"I remember Boo's Promise Celebration," said Charlie. "It was in here. It was like a really special party."

"I remember that!" said Vicky. "Some of the other Brownies helped to make the food."

"Food!" said Ellie, feeling hungry. "They got food too?"

"Yes!" Charlie laughed. "It was a proper party with balloons and food and everything!"

"I like the sound of that!" said Jamila, grinning.

"I'd like to do my Promise Celebration at the swimming pool – like Ellie's friend did," declared Katie. "It sounds really good fun."

"For you," agreed Grace thoughtfully. "But I'd like my Celebration to include some ballet. I could even make up a special Brownie dance."

"And I could make mine a music one!" said Jamila excitedly.

"Goodness, you've all got lots of great ideas," said Vicky. "What about you, Ellie, and Charlie? What kind of Celebrations do you think you'd like?"

"I don't know," said Ellie.

"Nor me," agreed Charlie. "Do we have to do one on our own? Perhaps me and Ellie could do ours together?"

"Of course," said Vicky. "Do you want some more time to think about it?"

But before the two friends could reply, Jamila interrupted.

"Hey," she said. "Are we being silly or what?"

"What do you mean?" replied Katie, with a puzzled look on her face.

"Well," said Jamila. "I know it would be cool for you to make your Promise at the swimming pool. And for Grace to do some ballet. But we're best friends, aren't we?"

The others nodded.

"And we joined Brownies together, didn't we?" Jamila pointed out.

"Oh, I get it!" said Ellie. "So we should all make our Promise together!"

"Of course!" grinned Grace. "That would be cool."

"But I want to make my Promise at the swimming pool!" Katie said again.

"Hands up who wants to make their Promise with Charlie and Ellie?" Jamila asked, putting up her hand.

Grace put her hand up too.

Katie gave a big sigh. Then she smiled. "You're right," she said, "we're best friends so we should make our Promise together."

"We could have one big party Celebration!" said Jamila.

The others nodded excitedly.

"So you'd all like to do the same thing?" Vicky asked.

"Yes, please!" they all shouted.

"A party it is then!" said Vicky. "And where would you like it? Here?"

The girls nodded again.

"Well, that's sorted!" said Vicky. "I'll ask some of the older Brownies if they would like to make some food. They can do that for their Hostess badge. And if you girls can make some invitations and give them to the people who you'd like to come, then our Celebration preparations have begun!"

The five best friends grinned, hugging each other in excitement. In just a couple of weeks' time, they would all be having their Promise Celebrations together!

The rest of the Brownie meeting just whizzed by. Finally, Vicky called everyone into a circle and collected up the signed permission letters for the trip to the Nature Centre the following week.

"Now," she said. "It's almost time to go and I can see lots of people waiting outside to take you home. Let's end our meeting by singing the Brownie Smile Song."

"Yeah!" the Brownies shouted and immediately began to sing:

I've got something in my pocket.
It belongs across my face,
And I keep it very close at hand
In a most convenient place.

Chapter 8

Over the next week, the five best friends seemed to talk about nothing but Brownies! If they weren't learning their Promise, or talking about their Promise Celebration party, they were in the playground at school playing the games that they had learned at Brownies. And when they weren't together, they were busy reading their *Becoming a Brownie* booklets and completing the puzzles.

On Thursday, the girls all went round to Ellie's house after school to make the invitations for their Promise Celebrations.

"I was going to invite Gran as well as Mum

and Dad," said Charlie, as she coloured in some green grass on the front of her invitation, "but she lives too far away to come..."

"Oh, you can share my granny!" Jamila hugged her friend. "But my brothers are definitely not coming. They'd just be really embarrassing!" She leaned over to borrow the blue felt tip and caught sight of Ellie's invites.

"Wow, Ellie! You're so good at drawing," sighed Jamila. "I wish I could draw like you."

"Thanks," said Ellie, blushing. "Yours are great, too. Everyone's had such brilliant ideas."

Daisy had suggested that they should decorate their invitations with pictures of things they liked doing. So Grace had drawn dancers on hers and Katie had been cutting out pictures of swimmers to stick on the ones she was making. Jamila had drawn pictures of musical instruments and music notes on hers. Ellie's were covered in illustrations of paintbrushes and pencils and Charlie had drawn her guinea pig, Nibbles, with a speech bubble coming out

of his mouth, saying "Charlie's Promise Celebration!"

"Do you think we can get them finished today?" asked Grace. "I can't wait to hand them out."

"As long as we do a little less talking and a bit more drawing," said Charlie, giggling.

The girls worked on quietly, and by the time Ellie's mum called them down for tea, they all had a beautiful set of invitations ready to hand out.

"Here, Mum, you can be the first," said Ellie, proudly handing her mum one of her invites.

"Oh, Ellie, it's lovely," said Mum, opening it up to look inside. "And I shall be delighted to join all of you at your Promise Celebration!"

"This is going to be the best Promise Celebration ever!" said Katie proudly.

On Sunday, Jamila's mum had promised to help them bake some cakes for their Promise Celebration party.

"We're going to make flapjacks," she said, as the girls gathered in the kitchen. "We can freeze them so they stay fresh for the party."

"Can I stir the mixture?" asked Ellie.

"You all can!" said Jamila's mum.

So together they weighed the ingredients, put them into the mixing bowl and took it in turns to stir the mixture. Then they poured it into the baking tin and Jamila's mum popped the tin into the oven. After a few minutes, a delicious smell started to spread across the kitchen.

"Yummy!" said Katie.

"I'm starving!" declared Jamila.

The others laughed.

"You're always hungry!" giggled Charlie.

"Would you like to decorate some biscuits while we're waiting for the flapjacks to cook?" asked Jamila's mum. "I've got some of that writing icing."

"Yeah!" squealed all the girls together.

"Are these for our party too?" Grace wanted to know.

"I thought you might want them now," said Jamila's mum, smiling. "We could make some more next week for the party."

"Yum!" said Jamila.

"Hey – why don't we use the icing to decorate the biscuits with pictures and words about Brownies?" suggested Ellie.

"Like the pictures on our Six badges?" asked Katie.

"Yes," said Grace.

"And we could write things like I LOVE BROWNIES!" added Charlie.

So that's what the five best friends did. Soon they had a table of beautiful Brownie biscuits. At first they didn't want to spoil their designs by eating them, but they were soon tucking in!

At last it was Tuesday night, and time for the trip to the Nature Centre! Jamila, Charlie, Ellie, Grace and Katie turned up in their waterproof coats, eager to get going.

"First, let's make sure everyone's here," said Sam. She called out the names of all the Brownies on her list, ticking them off as she went. "Excellent. Right, have you all got your coats? A pencil? Good. We've got two parents helping us this evening – Molly's auntie, Sian, and Sukia's mum, Nida. Is everyone ready?" Sam asked. "OK, let's go! And remember – you must behave like Brownies, as you are representing all Brownies everywhere when you are out and about."

"That reminds me!" Vicky said. "Out and about. Is there anyone here who has already done their Out and about badge?"

Amy put up her hand.

"Amy, of course you have!" Vicky smiled. "I wondered if the rest of you would like to use tonight's visit to the Nature Centre as a chance to start your Out and about badge?"

There was a buzz of excitement in the room.

"Part of the badge," Vicky explained, "is to do some map reading. And another part is to do a scavenger hunt! And Amy – as you are the Out and about expert, perhaps you could help some of the other Brownies?"

Amy grinned. "Of course!" she said.

"Right then!" Sam smiled. "Hedgehogs go with Nida, please, Rabbits with Sian, Badgers with Daisy, Squirrels with Vicky and Foxes with me. Have fun, everyone!"

Before they set off, each of the Sixes was given a list that said **SCAVENGER HUNT** at the top. It had names of things to find on their way to the Nature Centre.

"When you find any of the items on the list, you must tick them off," Vicky said. "But make sure you stick with your Six and don't wander off on your own."

The Brownies were busy reading their lists.

"I've got the first one!" whispered Izzy to the other Badgers. "A road sign – there's one over there! It says 'GIVE WAY'!"

The Badgers ticked it off their list, wrote down where they'd seen it and moved on.

"Do you think we get a prize if we get to the Nature Centre first?" Jamila asked.

"I don't know," said Holly. "But quick! The Foxes have already found three things! I can see over their shoulders – come on!"

In the Squirrels, Ashvini turned out to be really fast at spotting things. She even managed to spot a cat sitting on the roof of a garage for the clue that said "Four Legs and Furry". She saw it way before the others could even work out what the clue meant.

The Hedgehogs got to the Nature Centre first, although they were only just ahead of the other Sixes.

"Great!" Vicky said, collecting everyone's Scavenger Hunt lists. "It looks like you found everything! Now, Sam's going to hand out the nature trail list. This time you have to collect some of the items. But some things will be too big to pick up – or they might even be moving! So DON'T collect those!"

The Brownies looked at each other in surprise. What could be *moving*?

"If the item is moving, do a drawing of it on the back of your sheet and write down where you saw it," Vicky looked around at all the Brownies. "OK? Off you go then!"

The list had all sorts of things on it:

BADENBRIDGE NATURE CENTRE
NATURE TRAIL

1. Collect two leaves of different shapes.
2. Find a frog.
3. Seek out something with feathers.
4. Look in the water and what do you see?
5. How many different insects can you find?
6. Does anything have four legs?
7. Draw a plant.
8. Have you been amazed?

The Sixes scattered in different directions.

"What's going to have four legs?" Grace asked Boo.

"No idea," she said. "Maybe it's another cat? But what would that be doing here?"

Just then, the Brownies heard a strange noise. It sounded a bit like someone blowing a raspberry!

"What's that?" asked Caitlin.

"I think it came from behind those trees," Molly said. "Let's take a look."

The Rabbits followed their Sixer and found themselves near a fence.

"What's over there?" Lucy asked.

"Something with four legs!" said Grace and Molly at the same time.

"It's a gorgeous pony!" Boo exclaimed.

"And look at this," said Caitlin, picking up something in the grass. "It's a different kind of leaf from the ones over there!"

"That's two things we can tick off our list already," said Grace.

"And one we can take with us!" said Boo.

"But there's still lots more to go," said Molly. "Come on!"

The Squirrels were puzzling over the clue about water.

"Where is the water?" Ashvini asked.

"Perhaps there's a drinking fountain?" Bethany suggested.

"But we wouldn't be able to look into that," Megan pointed out.

"Maybe there's a pond?" Charlie wondered aloud.

"Good idea!" said Faith. "But where?"

The Squirrels looked around for clues.

"There!" said Megan. She was pointing over towards a signpost. "Follow that sign!"

A few minutes later, the Squirrels found themselves next to a pond.

"Make sure you stand back from the edge," Vicky said to the Brownies. Like all the other helpers, Vicky couldn't give the Brownies any help with their clues.

"What is there to see?" Charlie asked as she peeped into the water. "I can't see anything."

"There must be something!" said Ashvini.

"All I can see is us," said Faith.

"Us?" Megan didn't understand.

"Our reflections," said Charlie. "Of course!"

"Oh!" said Ashvini. "It's like that story you once told us, Vicky. You remember, Faith – the one about how Brownies got their name? Err, Twist me… umm … something about looking in the water?"

"Yes!" said Faith and Megan. "*Twist me and turn me and show me the elf. I looked in the water and there saw myself!*"

The girls quickly wrote down *Brownies* as their answer.

"But there must be something else in the pond," said Megan. "Surely?" She carried on looking. Something went *plip*!

"A FROG!" the Brownies all called out at once.

"Shush," Ashvini warned. "Don't give the answers away to the others!"

"Quick," said Megan. "Let's get drawing!"

The girls stood in silence as they tried to draw the frog quickly, before he hopped away.

"Come on!" urged Charlie. "We've still got loads to do!"

"We've finished!" declared Jessica, the Sixer of the Foxes.

"YES!" said Katie triumphantly.

"Well done," said Sam. "Right, let's all go over to the meeting point."

The Foxes walked back to the Visitor's Centre. They were amazed to find that the Badgers were already there with Daisy.

"We finished first!" Jamila smiled at Katie. "Did you find it hard?"

"No – dead easy," Katie said. Then she lowered her voice and whispered to Jamila. "Actually, I finished way before the others in my Six, but I had to stay and help them."

"I don't think it matters who got here first," said Jamila. "It's just for fun."

The other Sixes arrived shortly afterwards, excitedly swapping stories about the nature trail. Just then, a man appeared carrying a large camera. He had a badge on his jacket that said "The Badenbridge Reporter".

"That man's from the local newspaper!" Ellie pointed out to her friends.

"What's he doing here?" Grace wondered.

But before anyone could think of an answer, Vicky put up her right hand. Instantly, the Brownies fell silent.

"Brownies," she said, "have you had a good time?"

"Yes!" they all called out.

"I can see that you've all been very busy and that you've worked hard on your nature

trail," Vicky continued. "It'll soon be time to go back to the hall but before we do, I'd like to introduce Steven Hunt from the Badenbridge Reporter. He'd like to take a photo of the First Badenbridge Brownies for an article about the Nature Centre to go in next week's paper!"

"How cool is that!" said Jamila, grinning at her four best friends.

"Imagine, we're going to be in the paper!" Charlie exclaimed.

"Just wait till I tell my mum," said Ellie.

"Hi, Brownies!" said Steven. "If you'd all like to follow me, I'm going to take your photo in the Visitor's Centre."

The girls trooped inside.

"Hey, look!" said Charlie, pointing to a big, colourful display on the wall. "It's our bookmarks!"

"They look amazing!" declared Jamila.

All the Brownies raced over to see if they could find their own bookmarks. It was the perfect backdrop for the photo!

After lots of giggling and swapping places, the photograph was finally taken. Then the tired and happy Brownies walked back to the hall to meet their parents.

"It's your Promise Celebration party next week, isn't it," said Sam, as Ellie, Jamila, Charlie, Katie and Grace were leaving. "I hope you've all learned your Promise and Brownie Guide Law for it – see you next week!"

Chapter 9

"I think I know my Promise back to front and upside down as well!" Katie sighed.

It was Thursday after school, and Jamila, Ellie, Grace, Katie and Charlie had got together at Ellie's house to check that they were ready for their Promise Celebration the following week.

"I'm not sure I do," said Charlie. Having to say her Promise out loud still worried her.

"Come on," smiled Jamila kindly. "Let's see if we can do it together now!"

The five Brownies stood up and made the Brownie sign with their right hands.

I promise that I will do my best:
To love my God,
To serve the Queen and my country,
To help other people
And to keep the Brownie Guide Law.

"Phew!" Charlie exclaimed when they were finished. "I did it!"

"See!" said Jamila. "We knew you could!"

"Thanks," said Charlie gratefully. "I can't wait for next Tuesday. Boo's making a cake for our party."

"Scrummy!" said Ellie.

"And she said lots of the other Brownies are making cookies and sandwiches too."

"Is Boo doing her Hostess badge?" Katie asked.

"Yes, there are three girls doing it,"

Charlie explained. "And they're helping Vicky and Sam to decorate the hall too!"

"Boo's got loads of badges, hasn't she?" Grace sighed. "She's, like, one of the busiest Brownies!"

"Just like we'll be!" Katie pointed out.

"And only next week!" Jamila agreed.

The days flew by, with the five friends decorating more Brownie biscuits and practising saying their Promise.

Finally, it was the night of the Promise Celebration. The girls were looking extra smart in their Brownie clothes. They'd all made especially sure that their shoes were clean, and their hair was ultra neat.

Vicky asked for friends and family to come at the beginning of the Brownie meeting, so that the girls could carry on with their party after the Celebration was over.

"I'm so nervous!" said Jamila. She was unable to keep still for excitement.

"Me too!" said Katie and Grace together.

The hall was looking fantastic with balloons and streamers and posters giving the names of the Sixes, as well as some with the names of the five newest Brownies.

"Wow!" the girls sighed when they saw it.

Vicky and Sam had put out some chairs at one end of the hall and they were filling up with mums, dads and other members of the girls' families. Daisy and some of the older Brownies were handing out cups of tea and coffee and delicious things to eat.

The five best friends gathered over in the far corner of the Brownie hall with their Sixers. They looked, and felt, nervous.

"You'll be fine," Izzy smiled at them.

"It'll be fun!" grinned Lauren.

The room fell to a hush as Sam and Vicky put up their right hands.

"Ready, Brownies?" Vicky asked. "Good. Let's start our ceremony. Tonight, girls, we have five new Brownies who would like to join us, so we have a busy evening ahead. Let's start with our first one. Megan – as Sixer of the Squirrels, would you like to present your new Brownie, please."

"Come on!" Megan smiled at Charlie.

She was going first! The two girls skipped over to the Brownie Ring, where all the other Brownies had gathered with Sam, Vicky and Daisy.

"Hello, Megan. Who's this?" asked Vicky.

"This is Charlie and she would like to be a Brownie!"

Vicky asked Charlie if she knew her Brownie Law. She did!

Phew! Charlie thought to herself after she'd said it.

Her four best friends smiled encouragingly at her.

Vicky asked Charlie a few more questions about being a Brownie and then said, "Now, would you like to say your Brownie

Promise, Charlie?" Vicky held up her hand in the special Brownie sign.

Charlie nodded, put up her right hand like Vicky, gulped and began.

"I promise that I will..."

Charlie stopped. She couldn't think of the next word! She thought she knew it!

"Why don't you try again?" said Vicky gently.

But now Charlie couldn't even remember the first line!

"Don't worry," said Vicky, smiling kindly. "Would you like all the other Brownies to join in while you say your Promise?"

"Yes, please," whispered Charlie shyly.

So that's what the 1st Badenbridge Brownies did.

A short while later, Jamila, Katie, Ellie and Grace had all made their Brownie Promises too. When each of them had finished, Vicky shook their hands and gave them their special Brownie Promise badges. Now all five of them were proper Brownies!

"Well, I am very excited that we have so

many great new Brownies," Vicky said. "If you'd like to go over to see Sam and Daisy, they will give you your Celebration Certificates and Brownie Promise boxes."

"Thanks!" they all said and rushed over.

"What's in this?" Jamila asked, opening the yellow box she'd been given.

"Your copy of *Brownie Adventure*," said Daisy. "And the *Brownie Badge Book*."

"And here are your unit and district badges," said Sam, handing them all some cloth badges. "You'll need to get these sewn on to your sashes or tops so that everyone knows which Brownie unit you belong to."

"And these are your Six badges," explained Daisy. "You'll need those sewn on too!"

Chapter 10

The five best friends rushed over to their parents to show them their special presents.

"You'd better give those badges to me before they get lost," Charlie's dad said.

"You were all so great," said Jamila's mum. "Look at you – Brownies!"

"Here's my certificate!" said Ellie to her mum. "It says my name, and the date!"

"Well done, sweetheart," smiled her mum. "I'm very proud of you."

"Come on – photo!" said Katie and Grace's mum. "Let's get you all together on this very important occasion."

The new Brownies huddled together.

"Ready? Say CHEESE!" said the adults.

"BROWNIES!" shouted all the new Brownies at once before collapsing into giggles.

After all the mums and dads had left, the Brownie meeting continued with a brilliant party. The Brownies played some games and sang some favourite songs, before tucking into all the scrummy food. After everything had been cleared away, Vicky called everyone into the Brownie Ring.

"We don't have very much time left," Sam explained, "but we have got some more badges to hand out."

"Yes," said Vicky. "Boo, Holly and Bethany. I'd like to present you with your Hostess badges. You've all worked very hard over the last term preparing for it and finally making lovely decorations and food for this evening. Well done."

The Brownies, especially Katie, Jamila, Charlie, Grace and Ellie, all clapped them as they collected their badges.

"We also have three other presentations to make," Sam announced.

The Brownies exchanged puzzled looks.

"You'll all remember that you made bookmarks for the Nature Centre?" Vicky asked. "Well, the staff there have chosen three of their favourites. And the artists are ... Jessica, Jasmine and Ellie! Congratulations! You all get a free ticket to visit the centre with a friend!"

"That's brilliant, Ellie!" said Jamila, who had rushed over from the other side of the Brownie Ring to give her friend a hug.

"And finally," Sam said, "you remember having your photo taken last week?"

The Brownies certainly did!

"Well – before you go, take a look at the noticeboard and see if you can spot yourself on the front page of this week's paper!"

"Wow!" exclaimed all the girls, before they rushed over to take a peek.

Katie and Grace arrived in the school playground the next morning to find that the others were already there.

"My name's Charlie and I'm a Brownie!" said Charlie, rushing over to them.

"And we're Brownies too!" said Katie.

"Brownies Lend a Hand!" said Ellie.

"Brownies do a Good Turn!" added Jamila.

"Brownies do their Best!" smiled Charlie.

"Brownies ARE the best!" giggled Grace.

"YEAH!" agreed the five best friends all together.

1. Spent fifteen minutes a day for a week in Gran's garden, watching the birds. Made one of Gran's bird cakes.

2. Learned to recognize three wild birds, three butterflies and three mammals.

3. Asked Dad to help me make a hedgehog feeding station.

4. Went back to Badenbridge Nature Centre with Mum and Dad. Drew pictures of four different types of trees. Collected fallen leaves, made leaf rubbings and labelled them. Made bark rubbings and labelled them too.

Wildlife explorer